"VAN GOOL'S"

The Little Mermaid

TWIN BOOKS

Once upon a time, deep under the sea, there was a beautiful castle. Never had a ship's anchor touched it's roof it was so deep. The courtyard was full of unusual graceful flowers and algae where the fish came and went like flocks of birds in the sky.

This edition produced
for Book Express

© 1992 TWIN BOOKS UK Ltd

Produced by Twin Books
Kimbolton House
117A Fulham Road
London SW3 6RL

Directed by CND – Muriel Nathan-Deiller
Illustrated by Van Gool-Lefevre-Loisseaux

ISBN 185469-958 X

Printed in Hong Kong

This was the home of a King and Queen of the sea. They had five sprightly mermaid daughters.

"Oh! What a beauty! Give it to me!" Called one of them, laughing.

The mermaids were enjoying their favorite game, catching jellyfish. The mermaids' graceful beauty and elegance surpassed that of any creature outside the sea.

Having played for a while, the mermaids begged their father yet again; "Please, let us visit the world above."

The King frowned. "No, not until you are fifteen!" he said firmly. "I know you can't wait to see the sky with your own eyes, but it's much too dangerous!"

"Up above", added the Queen, "there is no water and people walk about with legs."
The youngest, prettiest and most inquisitive little mermaid listened intently. She loved her mother's tales about the world above.

"How beautiful the sea looks when the sun shines brightly from above!" sighed the youngest mermaid. "How I long to be fifteen."

And every day, the Little Mermaid would swim near the surface to watch the sun rays filtering through the water.

The mermaids waited, restless but obedient, for their chance to venture to the surface of the sea. The months passed slowly, but finally the eldest turned fifteen.

She chattered excitedly after her long-awaited trip. "The moon shines in the shape of a crescent!" she told her sisters. "Mother had said so, but I never imagined it could be so pretty."

A long year passed, and the second
mermaid turned fifteen. Her turn had
come to swim to the surface.

"The colors are like magic," she said
when she returned, her eyes shining
brightly.

But the Little Mermaid had a few more years to wait. She would sit restlessly at the foot of a statue, in a corner of the courtyard. It was the statue of a man from the world above.

"They stand on two feet?" she whispered to herself in wonder. "How come they don't fall over?"

On her first trip to the surface, the third mermaid saw human beings swimming at the mouth of a river.

"On land they manage very well," she told her sisters, laughing. "But in the water they're very clumsy?"

The fourth mermaid couldn't resist a cry of admiration when her turn finally came, and she caught a glimpse of the night sky. "There are thousands of stars glittering up above," she reported happily.

"Will I ever have a chance to discover anything as beautiful?" wondered the Little Mermaid impatiently.

At last it was the Little Mermaid's turn to emerge from the kingdom of the sea. It was sunset. She gazed in wonder and delight at a ship sailing gracefully through the ocean swells. The deck was brightly lit and she could hear music. The mermaid was so intrigued she swam closer to the boat.

A big wave lifted her up so she could see the ship's deck. People were talking, laughing and dancing. When a young man appeared, the music stopped abruptly and everyone cheered.

"Happy Birthday! Long live our prince!" shouted the people merrily.

"Thank you, my friends!" called the prince. "I shall never forget my fifteenth birthday!"

The party resumed, with singing and merriment.

23

The mermaid watched the handsome prince so
intently that she didn't notice the storm approaching.
The gentle breeze became a whistling gale, whipping
the sea into giant waves. The music stopped and
deckhands rushed about as the ship rose and fell on
the angry ocean. Suddenly the great mast snapped and
the ship rolled sideways. Water rushed on to the deck.

Sea and wind tore at the sinking ship.
The Little Mermaid watched in horror as
the prince was swept into the water. He
struggled to swim, but pounding waves
pushed him under.

"No!" cried the mermaid, swimming
swiftly to him. She pulled him by his coat
collar back to the surface. She had never
imagined she would have such strength.

The Little Mermaid swam a long way, holding the prince in her arms. His eyes were closed. When she reached the shore, she lay him on the sand. She was exhausted. Catching her breath, she smoothed back his hair and gently kissed his cheek. Then, in her beautiful voice, she began singing an old mermaid tune to his ear to awaken him.

The prince stirred, blinking his eyes and trying to focus.

Just then three young girls came running from the nearby castle. The Little Mermaid slipped back into the sea, relieved that the prince was out of danger, but her heart was full of sorrow.

Deep down in the sea, the Little Mermaid no longer sat by the statue. Clutched in her hand, she held a piece of fabric which had been torn off the prince's coat in the shipwreck. "I wish I could see this handsome young man again," she thought. Her parents wondered why was she so unhappy. She told them nothing about her trip to the surface.

At last, she decided she must somehow join him. "But how will I be able to walk without legs?" she wondered. Then she thought of the sea witch. "She's the only one who can help me!" she said excitedly.

The Little Mermaid swam a long way until she reached the dark waters that were the witch's domain. She found the witch hiding under the tentacles of an octopus. The mermaid was so afraid she couldn't speak.

"I know what you want, little one!" said the witch, glaring at her. "Two lovely legs to run about with! I can do that for you. But you must give me something in return." The witch paused a moment, then continued, "would you give your beautiful voice?"

The Little Mermaid didn't think twice. She would have done anything to join her prince. "Yes" she cried.

No sooner had she spoken the word than her voice was gone. Unable to utter a sound the mermaid sadly touched her throat.

"Take this potion and go to the kingdom of human beings," said the witch. When you drink it your mermaid tail will separate. It will be painful then but you will have the most beautiful legs of Earth!"

The Little Mermaid took the potion and swam quickly to the surface. She made her way to the shore near the prince's castle.

"The witch said it would hurt," she thought, hesitating for a moment. But remembering how miserable she had been at the bottom of the sea, far away from the one she loved, she gathered her courage and drank the potion.

The Little Mermaid felt as if her body were being sliced in half. And before she knew whether the magic had succeeded, she fainted on the sand.

When she awoke, not only did she have two lovely legs, but he was there, the handsome young man she had rescued from the shipwreck, the prince charming she had held in her arms.

"You're opening your eyes at last!" he said softly. "I was so worried when I found you unconscious."

The prince handed her some clothes and helped her to stand up. It wasn't easy! He thought she was dizzy because she was weak. But she was painfully learning to walk.

That night a ball was held at the castle. The beautiful, silent Little Mermaid danced happily with the prince. No one knew who she was, or what pain she felt for having those dainty legs.

Time went by and the Little Mermaid suffered in silence. But the prince was so kind to her that she almost forgot the pain. She wished she could tell him her story, and hoped he could see the love in her eyes. But one day, she heard that he was about to marry the young girl who had found him on the beach. "He thinks she's the one who rescued him!" thought the mermaid desperately. "He doesn't love me!"

Ever since the Little Mermaid had left the kingdom of the sea, her sisters had visited her each day. Unable to talk, she made gestures to explain how desperate she was.

"I know," said the eldest, "the prince doesn't love her. We must help our dear sister. Let's ask the witch! If we give her our beautiful long hair, she may agree to help our sister again."

The mermaid sisters went to the witch with their request.

"No girls," was the witch's reply. "Keep your hair. I am not as cruel as you think, and I know what is going on up there. Your brave little sister has earned the right to be happy. Take this potion to her. She will recover her voice, and her beloved prince will be able to follow her deep down into the world of the sea!"

The prince's wedding ceremony on the royal ship had begun when the Little Mermaid drank some of the liquid potion and began to sing:

> *"My heart is full of sorrow*
> *For you have forgotten*
> *The song of the mermaids*
> *I whispered in your ear."*

The prince suddenly turned around. His heart filled with love as he gazed at the Little Mermaid and listened to her sweet voice.

The prince listened in awe while the mermaid sang the story of all that had happened because of her love for him.

"You're the one who rescued me!" he said. "And ever since, your song has been with me. At night a mermaid was singing in my dreams. It was you!" The Little Mermaid was overjoyed and she held out the potion. "Drink this, my prince," she whispered. "If you love me, you'll sacrifice your world, as I did my voice."

Looking straight into the Little Mermaid's eyes, the prince took the potion and drank it down.

"Follow me to my kingdom," said the mermaid, smiling radiantly.

Together they dove into the deep blue sea.

The Little Mermaid could hardly contain her happiness. What a pleasure it was to be swimming again and to be with her beloved prince! Thousands of silver bubbles popped up to the surface, saying farewell to the world above.

Hand in hand the prince and the Little Mermaid swam gracefully together with a ballet of multicolored fish.

"See how peaceful and gentle life is down here?" exclaimed the mermaid, laughing.

Still wearing their wedding finery the happy couple made their way to the King and Queen's castle at the bottom of the sea. They were followed by the mermaids.

The mermaid's mother and father were overjoyed to have their daughter back. They listened to the Little Mermaid's story, then the King turned to the young man. "Welcome!" he exclaimed. "We wish you happiness! Fish tails or naked feet, love is the only thing that counts!"

The King of the sea hosted a big wedding ceremony. The young couple then left in a beautiful carriage, pulled by four seahorses. The mermaid's family bade them goodbye from the steps, wishing them eternal happiness.

A cheer went up as the carriage started off.
Every one of the King's subjects waved and
threw kisses as they went by. They could see
the beautiful love between the Little
Mermaid and her prince.

And when the new couple's honeymoon
was over, the prince and the Little Mermaid
returned to the castle under the sea where
they lived happily ever after.